THE DIARY OF
ANNE RODWAY

BY

WILKIE COLLINS

British Library Cataloguing-in-Publication Data
A catalogue record for this book is available from the
British Library

CONTENTS

WILKIE COLLINS

William Wilkie Collins was born in Marylebone, London in 1824. His family enrolled him at the Maida Hill Academy in 1835, but then took him to France and Italy with them between 1836 and 1838. Collins later recalled that in Italy he learned more "which has been of use to me, among the scenery, the pictures, and the people, than I ever learned at school." Returning to England, Collins attended Cole's boarding school, and completed his education in 1841, after which he was apprenticed to the tea merchants Antrobus & Co. in the Strand.

In 1846, Collins became a law student at Lincoln's Inn, and was called to the bar in 1851, although he never practiced. It was in 1848, a year after the death of his father, that he published his first book, *The Memoirs of the Life of William Collins, Esq., R.A.*, to good reviews. This was followed by an historical novel, *Antonina* (1850) and three contemporary novels, *Basil* (1852), *Hide and Seek* (1854) and *The Dead Secret* (1857). During the 1850s, however, Collins' main source of income came through journalism. Primarily, he wrote for *Household Words*, a publication owned and ran by Charles Dickens, with whom Collins had a close friendship. It was also during this decade that Collins began to take large amounts of opium to combat 'rheumatic gout', a form of arthritis he suffered from.

The 1860s saw Collins' creative high-point, and it was during this decade that he achieved fame and critical acclaim, with his four major novels, *The Woman in White* (1860), *No Name* (1862), *Armadale* (1866) and *The Moonstone* (1868). These were all hugely popular; *The Woman in White*, for example, ran to seven editions in the first year of publication, and is now regarded as the archetypal sensation novel. *The Moonstone*, meanwhile is seen by many as the first true detective novel–T. S. Eliot called it "the first, the longest, and the best of modern English detective novels . . . in a genre invented by Collins and not by Poe."

During the last two decades of his life, Collins' popularity waned. This was due in part to the death of Dickens, and in part to his increasing dependence on opium. It also had a lot to do with his stylistic shift away from the sensational thrillers that his made his name onto works more centred on social commentary; *Jezebel's Daughter* (1880), for example, advocated humane treatment of lunatics, whilst *Heart and Science* (1883) condemned vivisection. During the 1880s, Collins' health declined rapidly. In June of 1889, Collins suffered a stroke, and died as a result of further complications three months later, aged 65.

THE DIARY OF ANNE RODWAY

WILKIE COLLINS

[Taken from her Diary]

MARCH 3RD, 1840. A long letter to-day from Robert, which surprised and vexed me so that I have been sadly behindhand with my work ever since. He writes in worse spirits than last time, and absolutely declares that he is poorer even than when he went to America, and that he has made up his mind to come home to London.

How happy I should be at this news, if he only returned to me a prosperous man! As it is, although I love him dearly, I cannot look forward to the meeting him again, disappointed and broken down, and poorer than ever, without a feeling almost of dread for both of us. I was twenty-six last birthday, and he was thirty-three, and there seems less chance now than ever of our being married. It is all I can do to keep myself by my needle, and his prospects, since he failed in the small stationery business three years ago, are worse, if possible, than mine.

Not that I mind so much for myself: women, in all ways of life, and especially in my dressmaking way, learn, I think, to be more patient than men. What I dread is Robert's despondency and the hard struggle he will have in this cruel city to get his bread–let alone making money enough to marry me. So little as poor people want to set up in housekeeping and be happy together, it seems hard that they can't get it when they are honest and hearty and willing to work. The clergyman said in his sermon last Sunday evening, that all things are ordered for the best and we are all put into the stations in life that are properest for us. I suppose he was right, being a very clever gentleman who fills the church to crowding, but I think I should have understood him better if I had not been very hungry at the time, in consequence of my own station in life being nothing but Plain Needlewoman.

MARCH 4TH.

Mary Mallinson came down to my room to take a cup of tea with me. I read her bits of Robert's letter to show her that, if she has her troubles, I have mine, too. But I could not succeed in cheering her. She says she is born to misfortune and that, as long back as she can remember, she has never had the least morsel of luck to be thankful for. I told her to go and look in my glass, and to say if she had nothing to be thankful for then, for Mary is a very pretty girl, and would look still prettier if she could be more cheerful and dress neater. However, my compliment did no good. She rattled her spoon impatiently in her teacup, and said:

"If I was only as good a hand at needlework as you are, Anne, I would change faces with the ugliest girl in London."

"Not you!" says I, laughing. She looked at me for a moment and shook her head, and was out of the room before I could get up and stop her. She always runs off in that way when she is going to cry, having a kind of pride about letting other people see her in tears.

MARCH 5TH.

A fright about Mary. I had not seen her all day, as she does not work at the same place where I do, and in the evening she never came down to have tea with me, or sent me word to go to her. So just before I went to bed, I ran upstairs to say good-night.

She did not answer when I knocked, and, when I stepped softly into the room, I saw her in bed, asleep, with her work not half done, lying about the room in the untidiest way. There was nothing remarkable in that, and I was just going away on tip-toe, when a tiny bottle and wineglass on the chair by her bed-side caught my eye. I thought she was ill, and had been taking physic, and looked at the bottle. It was marked in large letters: "Laudanum–Poison".

My heart gave a jump, as if it was going to fly out of me. I laid hold of her with both hands, and shook her with all my might. She was sleeping heavily, and woke slowly, as it seemed to me–but still she did wake. I tried to pull her out of bed, having heard that people ought to be always walked up and down when they have taken laudanum, but she resisted and pushed me away violently.

"Anne!" says she, in a fright. "For gracious sake, what's come to you? Are you out of your senses?"

"Oh, Mary! Mary!" says I, holding up the bottle before her, "if I hadn't come in when I did–" And I laid hold of her to shake her again.

She looked puzzled at me for a moment, then smiled (the first time I had seen her do so for many a long day), then put her arms round my neck.

"Don't be frightened about me, Anne," she says. "I am not worth it, and there is no need."

"No need!" says I, out of breath. "No need, when the bottle has got Poison marked on it!"

"Poison, dear, if you take it all," says Mary, looking at me very tenderly, "and a night's rest, if you only take a little."

I watched her for a moment, doubtful whether I ought to believe what she said, or to alarm the house. But there was no sleepiness now in her eyes and nothing drowsy in her voice, and she sat up in bed quite easily, without anything to support her.

"You have given me a dreadful fright, Mary," says I, sitting down by her in the chair, and beginning, by this time, to feel rather faint after being startled so.

She jumped out of bed to get me a drop of water, and kissed me, and said how sorry she was, and how undeserving of so much interest being taken in her. At the same time, she tried to possess herself of the laudanum bottle, which I still kept cuddled up tight in my own hands.

"No," says I. "You have got into a low-spirited, despairing way. I won't trust you with it."

"I am afraid I can't do without it," says Mary, in her usual quiet, hopeless voice. "What with work that I can't get through as I ought, and troubles that I can't help thinking of, sleep won't come to me unless I take a few drops out of that bottle. Don't keep it away from me, Anne. It's the only thing in the world that makes me forget myself."

"Forget yourself!" says I. "You have no right to talk in that way, at your age. There's something horrible in the notion of a girl of eighteen sleeping with a bottle of laudanum by her bedside every night. We all of us have our troubles. Haven't

I got mine?"

"You can do twice the work I can, twice as well as me," says Mary. "You are never scolded and rated at for awkwardness with your needle, and I always am. You can pay for your room every week, and I am three weeks in debt for mine."

"A little more practice", says I, "and a little more courage, and you will soon do better. You have got all your life before you—"

"I wish I was at the end of it," says she, breaking in. "I'm alone in the world, and my life's no good to me."

"You ought to be ashamed of yourself for saying so," says I. "Haven't you got me for a friend? Didn't I take a fancy to you when first you left your stepmother and came to lodge in this house, and haven't I been sisters with you ever since? Suppose you are alone in the world, am I much better off? I'm an orphan, like you. I've almost as many things in pawn as you; and if your pockets are empty, mine have only got nine-pence in them, to last me for all the rest of the week."

"Your father and mother were honest people," says Mary obstinately. "My mother ran away from home and died in a hospital. My father was always drunk and always beating me. My stepmother is as good as dead, for all she cares about me. My only brother is thousands of miles away, in foreign parts, and never writes to me, and never helps me with a farthing. My sweetheart . . ."

She stopped, and the red flew into her face. I knew, if she went on that way, she would only get to the saddest part of her sad story, and give both herself and me unnecessary pain.

"*My* sweetheart is too poor to marry me, Mary," I said, "so I'm not so much to be envied even there. But let's give over disputing which is worst off. Lie down in bed and let me tuck you up. I'll put a stitch or two into that work of yours while you go to sleep."

Instead of doing what I told her, she burst out crying (being very like a child in some of her ways) and hugged me so tight round the neck that she quite hurt me. I let her go on till she had worn herself out, and was obliged to lie down. Even then, her last few words, before she dropped off to sleep, were such as I was half sorry, half frightened, to hear.

"I won't plague you long, Anne," she said. "I haven't courage to go out of the world as you seem to fear I shall. But I began my life wretchedly, and wretchedly I am sentenced to end it."

It was of no use lecturing her again, for she closed her eyes.

I tucked her up as neatly as I could, and put her petticoat over her, for the bed-clothes were scanty and her hands felt cold. She looked so pretty and delicate as she fell asleep, that it quite made my heart ache to see her, after such talk as we had held together. I just waited long enough to be quite sure that she was in the land of dreams, then emptied the horrible laudanum bottle into the grate, took up her half-done work and, going out softly, left her for that night.

MARCH 6TH.

Sent off a long letter to Robert, begging and entreating him not to he so downhearted, and not to leave America without making another effort. I told him I could bear any trial except the wretchedness of seeing him come back a helpless, broken-down man, trying uselessly to begin life again, when too old for a change.

It was not till after I had posted my own letter and read over parts of Robert's again that the suspicion suddenly floated across me, for the first time, that he might have sailed for England immediately after writing to me. There were expressions in the letter which seemed to indicate that he had some such headlong project in his mind. And yet, surely, if it were so, I ought to have noticed them at the first reading. I can only hope I am wrong in my present interpretation of much of what he has written to me–hope it earnestly, for both our sakes.

This has been a doleful day for me. I have been uneasy about Robert and uneasy about Mary. My mind is haunted by those last words of hers: "I began my life wretchedly, and wretchedly I am sentenced to end it." Her usual melancholy way of talking never produced the same impression on me that I feel now. Perhaps the discovery of the laudanum bottle is the cause of this. I would give many a hard day's work to know what to do for Mary's good. My heart warmed to her when we first met in the same lodging-house two years ago, and, although I am not one of the over-affectionate sort myself, I feel as if I could go to the world's end to serve that girl. Yet, strange to say, if I was asked why I was so fond of her, I don't think I should know how to answer the question.

MARCH 7TH.

I am almost ashamed to write it down, even in this journal, which no eyes but mine ever look on; yet I must honestly confess to myself, that here I am, at nearly one in the morning, sitting up in a state of serious uneasiness, because Mary has not yet come home.

I walked with her this morning to the place where she works, and tried to lead her into talking of the relations she has got who are still alive. My motive in doing this was to see if she dropped anything in the course of conversation which might suggest a way of helping her interests with those who are bound to give her all reasonable assistance. But the little I could get her to say to me led to nothing. Instead of answering my questions about her stepmother and her brother, she persisted at first, in the strangest way, in talking of her father, who was dead and gone, and of one Noah Truscott, who had been the worst of all the bad friends he had, and had taught him to drink and game. When I did get her to speak of her brother, she only knew that he had gone out to a place called Assam, where they grew tea. How he was doing, or whether he was there still, she did not seem to know, never having heard a word from him for years and years past.

As for her stepmother, Mary, not unnaturally, flew into a passion the moment I spoke of her. She keeps an eating-house at Hammersmith, and could have given Mary good employment in it, but she seems always to have hated her and to have made her life so wretched with abuse and ill-usage that she had no refuge left but to go away from home and do her best to make a living for herself. Her husband (Mary's father) appears to have behaved badly to her, and, after his death, she took the wicked course of revenging herself on her stepdaughter. I felt, after this, that it was impossible Mary could go back, and that it was the hard necessity of her position, as it is of mine, that she should struggle on to make a decent livelihood without assistance from any of her relations. I confessed as much as this to her; but I added that I would try to get her employment with the persons for whom I work, who pay higher wages and show a little more indulgence to those under them than the people to whom she is now obliged to look for support.

I spoke much more confidently than I felt about being able to do this, and left her, as I thought, in better spirits than usual. She promised to be back to-night to tea, at nine o'clock, and now it is nearly one in the morning, and she is not home yet. If it was any other girl, I should not feel uneasy, for I should make up my mind that there was extra work to be done in a hurry, and that they were keeping her late and I should go to bed. But Mary is so unfortunate in everything that happens to her, and her own melancholy talk about herself keeps hanging on my mind so, that I have fears on her account which would not distress me about any one else. It seems inexcusably silly to think such a thing, much more to write it down; but I have a kind of nervous dread upon me that some accident–.

What does that loud knocking at the street door mean? And those voices and heavy footsteps outside? Some lodger who has lost his key, I suppose. And yet, my heart–What a coward I have become all of a sudden!

More knocking and louder voices. I must run to the door and see what it is. O Mary! Mary! I hope I am not going to have another fright about you; but I feel sadly like it.

MARCH 8TH.
MARCH 9TH.
MARCH 10TH.
MARCH 11TH.

O me! all the troubles I have ever had in my life are as nothing to the trouble I am in now. For three days I have not been able to write a single line in this journal, which I have kept so regularly ever since I was a girl. For three days I have not once thought of Robert–I, who am always thinking of him at other times.

My poor, dear, unhappy Mary! the worst I feared for you on that night when I sat up alone was far below the dreadful calamity that has really happened. How can I write about it, with my eyes full of tears and my hand all of a tremble? I don't even know why I am sitting down at my desk now, unless it is habit that keeps me to my old everyday task, in spite of the grief and fear which seem to unfit me entirely for performing it.

The people of the house were asleep and lazy on that dreadful night, and I was the first to open the door. Never, never could I describe in writing, or even say in plain talk, although it is so much easier, what I felt when I saw two policemen come in, carrying between them what seemed to me to be a dead girl, and that girl Mary! I caught hold of her, and gave a scream that must have alarmed the whole house; for frightened people came crowding downstairs in their night-dresses. There was a dreadful confusion and noise of loud talking, but I heard nothing, and saw nothing, till I had got her into my room, and laid on my bed. I stooped down, frantic-like, to kiss her, and saw an awful mark of a blow on the left temple, and felt, at the same time, a feeble flutter of her breath on my cheek. The discovery that she was not dead seemed to give me back my senses again. I told one of the policemen where the nearest doctor was to be found, and sat down by the bedside, while he was gone, and bathed her poor head with cold water. She never opened her eyes, or moved or spoke, but she breathed, and that was enough for me, because it was enough for life.

The policeman left in the room was a big, thick-voiced, pompous man, with a horrible unfeeling pleasure in hearing himself talk before an assembly of frightened, silent people. He told us how he had found her, as if he had been telling a story in a tap-room, and began with saying:

"I don't think the young woman was drunk."

Drunk! My Mary, who might have been a born lady for all the spirits she ever touched–drunk! I could have struck the man for uttering the word, with her lying, poor suffering angel, so white and still and helpless before him. As it was, I gave him a look; but he was too stupid to understand it, and went droning on, saying the same thing over and over again in the same words. And yet the story of how they found her was, like all the sad stories I have ever heard told in real life, so very, very short. They had just seen her lying along on the kerb-stone, a few streets off, and had taken her to the station-house. There she had been searched, and one of my cards, that I give to ladies who promise me employment, had been found in her pocket, and so they had brought her to our house. This was all the man really had to tell. There was nobody near her when she was found, and no evidence to show how the blow on her temple had been inflicted.

What a time it was before the doctor came, and how dreadful to hear him say, after he had looked at her, that he was afraid all the medical men in the world could be of no use here; he could not get her to swallow anything, and the more he tried to bring her back to her senses, the less chance there seemed of his succeeding. He examined the blow on her temple, and said he thought she must have fallen down in a fit of some sort and struck her head against the pavement, and so have given her brain what he was afraid was a fatal shake. I asked what was to be done if she showed any return to sense in the night. He said:

"Send for me directly," and stopped for a little while

afterwards, stroking her head gently with his hand, and whispering to himself: "Poor girl, so young and so pretty!" I had felt, some minutes before, as if I could have struck the policeman, and I felt now as if I could have thrown my arms round the doctor's neck and kissed him. I did put out my hand, when he took up his hat, and he shook it in the friendliest way.

"Don't hope, my dear," he said, and went out.

The rest of the lodgers followed him, all silent and shocked, except the inhuman wretch who owns the house and lives in idleness on the high rents he wrings from poor people like us.

"She's three weeks in my debt," says he, with a frown and an oath. "Where the devil is my money to come from now?"–Brute! brute!

I had a long cry alone with her, that seemed to ease my heart a little. She was not the least changed for the better when I had wiped away the tears and could see her clearly again. I took up her right hand, which lay nearest to me. It was tight clenched. I tried to unclasp the fingers, and succeeded after a little time. Something dark fell out of the palm of her hand as I straightened it.

I picked the thing up, and smoothed it out, and saw that it was an end of a man's cravat.

A very old, rotten, dingy strip of black silk, with thin lilac lines, all blurred and deadened with dirt, running across and across the stuff in a sort of trellis-work pattern. The small end of the cravat was hemmed in the usual way, but the other end was all jagged, as if the morsel then in my hands had been torn off violently from the rest of the stuff. A chill ran all over me as I looked at it, for that poor, stained, crumpled end of a cravat seemed to be saying to me, as though it had been in plain words—"If she dies, she has come to her death by foul means, and I am the witness of it."

I had been frightened enough before, lest she should die suddenly and quietly without my knowing it, while we were alone together; but I got into a perfect agony now, for fear this last worst affliction should take me by surprise. I don't suppose five minutes passed all that woeful night through, without my getting up and putting my cheek close to her mouth, to feel if the faint breaths still fluttered out of it. They came and went just the same as at first, although the fright I was in often made me fancy they were stilled for ever.

Just as the church clocks were striking four, I was startled by seeing the room door open. It was only Dusty Sal (as they call her in the house), the maid-of-all-work. She was wrapped up in the blanket off her bed, her hair was all tumbled over her face and her eyes were heavy with sleep, as she came up to the bedside where I was sitting.

"I've two hours good before I begin to work," says she, in her hoarse, drowsy voice, "and I've come to sit up and take my turn at watching her. You lay down and get some sleep on the rug. Here's my blanket for you–I don't mind the cold–it will keep me awake."

"You are very kind–very, very kind and thoughtful, Sally," says I, "but I am too wretched in my mind to want sleep or rest, or to do anything but wait where I am and try and hope for the best."

"Then I'll wait, too," says Sally. "I must do something; if there's nothing to do but waiting, I'll wait."

And she sat down opposite me at the foot of the bed, and drew the blanket close round her with a shiver.

"After working so hard as you do, I'm sure you must want all the little rest you can get," says I.

"Excepting only you," says Sally, putting her heavy arm very clumsily, but very gently at the same time, round Mary's feet, and looking hard at the pale still face on the pillow. "Excepting you, she's the only soul in this house as never swore at me or give me a hard word that I can remember. When you made puddings on Sundays and give her half, she always give me a bit. The rest of 'em calls me Dusty Sal. Excepting only you, again, she always called me Sally, as if she knowed me in a friendly way. I ain't no good here, but I ain't no harm neither, and I shall take my turn at the sitting

19

up—that's what I shall do!"

She nestled her head down close at Mary's feet as she spoke those words, and said no more. I once or twice thought she had fallen asleep, but whenever I looked at her, her heavy eyes were always wide open. She never changed her position an inch till the church clocks struck six; then she gave one little squeeze to Mary's feet with her arm, and shuffled out of the room without a word. A minute or two after, I heard her down below lighting the kitchen fire just as usual.

A little later, the doctor stepped over before his breakfast-time to see if there had been any change in the night. He only shook his head when he looked at her, as if there was no hope. Having nobody else to consult that I could put trust in, I showed him the end of the cravat, and told him of the dreadful suspicion that had arisen in my mind when I found it in her hand.

"You must keep it carefully, and produce it at the inquest," he said. "I don't know, though, that it is likely to lead to anything. The bit of stuff may have been lying on the pavement near her, and her hand may have unconsciously clutched it when she fell. Was she subject to fainting fits?"

"Not more so, sir, than other young girls who are hard-worked and anxious, and weakly from poor living," I answered.

"I can't say that she may not have got that blow from a

fall," the doctor went on, looking at her temple again. "I can't say that it presents any positive appearance of having been inflicted by another person. It will be important, however, to ascertain what state of health she was in last night. Have you any idea where she was yesterday evening?"

I told him where she was employed at work, and said I imagined she must have been kept there later than usual.

"I shall pass the place this morning," said the doctor, "in going my rounds among my patients, and I'll just step in and make some inquiries."

I thanked him, and we parted. Just as he was closing the door, he looked in again.

"Was she your sister?" he asked.

"No, sir, only my dear friend."

He said nothing more, but I heard him sigh, as he shut the door softly. Perhaps he once had a sister of his own and lost her. Perhaps she was like Mary in the face.

The doctor was hours gone away. I began to feel unspeakably forlorn and helpless. So much so, as even to wish selfishly that Robert might really have sailed from America, and might get to London in time to assist and console me.

No living creature came into the room but Sally. The first time she brought me some tea; the second and third times she only looked in to see if there was any change, and glanced her eye towards the bed. I had never known her so

21

silent before; it seemed almost as if this dreadful accident had struck her dumb. I ought to have spoken to her, perhaps, but there was something in her face that daunted me; and, besides, the fever of anxiety I was in began to dry up my lips, as if they would never be able to shape any words again. I was still tormented by that frightful apprehension of the past night, that Mary would die without my knowing it–die without saying one word to clear up the awful mystery of this blow and set the suspicions at rest for ever which I still felt whenever my eyes fell on the end of the old cravat.

At last the doctor came back.

"I think you may safely clear your mind of any doubts to which that bit of stuff may have given rise," he said. "She was, as you supposed, detained late by her employers, and she fainted in the work-room. They most unwisely and unkindly let her go home alone, without giving her any stimulant, as soon as she came to her senses again. Nothing is more probable, under these circumstances, than that she should faint a second time on her way here. A fall on the pavement, without any friendly arm to break it, might have produced even a worse injury than the injury we see. I believe that the only ill-usage to which the poor girl was exposed was the neglect she met with in the work-room."

"You speak very reasonably, I own, sir," said I, not yet quite convinced. "Still, perhaps she may–"

"My poor girl, I told you not to hope," said the doctor, interrupting me. He went to Mary and lifted up her eyelids and looked at her eyes while he spoke, then added: "If you still doubt how she came by that blow, do not encourage the idea that any words of hers will ever enlighten you. She will never speak again."

"Not dead! Oh! sir, don't say she's dead!"

"She is dead to pain and sorrow—dead to speech and recognition. There is more animation in the life of the feeblest insect that flies than in the life that is left in her. When you look at her now, try to think that she is in heaven. That is the best comfort I can give you, after telling the hard truth."

I did not believe him. I could not believe him. So long as she breathed at all, so long I was resolved to hope. Soon after the doctor was gone, Sally came in again and found me listening (if I may call it so) at Mary's lips. She went to where my little hand-glass hangs against the wall, took it down and gave it to me.

"See if the breath marks it," she said.

Yes; her breath did mark it, but very faintly. Sally cleaned the glass with her apron, and gave it back to me. As she did so, she half stretched out her hand to Mary's face, but drew it in again suddenly, as if she was afraid of soiling the delicate skin with her hard, horny fingers. Going out, she stopped at the foot of the bed, and scraped away a little patch of mud that was on one of Mary's shoes.

"I always used to clean 'em for her," said Sally, "to save her hands from getting blacked. May I take 'em off now, and clean 'em again?"

I nodded my head, for my heart was too heavy to speak. Sally took the shoes off with a slow, awkward tenderness, and went out.

An hour or more must have passed, when, putting the glass over her lips again, I saw no mark on it. I held it closer and closer. I dulled it accidentally with my own breath, and cleaned it. I held it over her again. Oh! Mary, Mary, the doctor was right! I ought to have only thought of you in heaven!

Dead, without a word, without a sign–without even a look to tell the true story of the blow that killed her! I could not call to anybody, I could not cry, I could not so much as put the glass down and give her a kiss for the last time. I don't know how long I had sat there with my eyes burning and my hands deadly cold, when Sally came in with the shoes cleaned, and carried carefully in her apron for fear of a soil touching them. At the sight of that–

I can write no more. My tears drop so fast on the paper that I can see nothing.

MARCH 12TH.

She died on the afternoon of the eighth. On the morning of the ninth, I wrote, as in duty bound, to her stepmother at Hammersmith. There was no answer. I wrote again; my letter was returned to me this morning, unopened. For all that woman cares, Mary might be buried with a pauper's funeral. But this shall never be, if I pawn everything about me, down to the very gown that is on my back.

The bare thought of Mary being buried by the workhouse gave me the spirit to dry my eyes and go to the undertaker's, and tell him how I was placed. I said, if he would get me an estimate of all that would have to be paid, from first to last, for the cheapest decent funeral that could be had, I would undertake to raise the money. He gave me the estimate, written in this way, like a common bill:

A walking funeral complete	£1 13 8
Vestry	0 4 4
Rector	0 4 4
Clerk	0 1 0
Sexton	0 1 0
Beadle	0 1 0
Bell	0 1 0
Six feet of ground	0 2 0
Total . .	£2 8 4

If I had the heart to give any thought to it, I should be inclined to wish that the Church could afford to do without so many small charges for burying poor people, to whose friends even shillings are of consequence. But it is useless to complain: the money must be raised at once. The charitable doctor–a poor man himself, or he would not be living in our neighbourhood–has subscribed ten shillings towards the expenses; and the coroner, when the inquest was over, added five more. Perhaps others may assist me. If not, I have fortunately clothes and furniture of my own to pawn. And I must set about parting with them without delay; for the funeral is to be to-morrow, the thirteenth.

The funeral–Mary's funeral! It is well that the straits and difficulties I am in, keep my mind on the stretch. If I had leisure to grieve, where should I find the courage to face to-morrow?

Thank God they did not want me at the inquest. The verdict given–with the doctor, the policeman and two persons from the place where she worked, for witnesses–was "Accidental Death". The end of the cravat was produced, and the coroner said that it was certainly enough to suggest suspicion, but the jury, in the absence of any positive evidence, held to the doctor's notion that she had fainted and fallen down, and so got the blow on her temple. They reproved the people where Mary worked for letting her go home alone, without so much as a drop of brandy to support her, after she had fallen into a swoon, from exhaustion, before their eyes. The coroner added, on his own account, that he thought the reproof was thoroughly deserved. After that, the cravat-end was given back to me, by my own desire, the police saying that they could make no investigations with such a slight clue to guide them. They may think so, and the coroner, and doctor, and jury may think so, but, in spite of all that has passed, I am now more firmly persuaded than ever that there is some dreadful mystery in connection with that blow on my poor lost Mary's temple which has yet to be revealed, and which may come to be discovered through this very fragment of a cravat that I found in her hand. I cannot give any good reason why I think so, but I know that if I had been one of the jury at the inquest, nothing should have induced me to consent to such a verdict as Accidental Death.

After I had pawned my things, and had begged a small advance of wages at the place where I work to make up what was still wanting to pay for Mary's funeral, I thought I might have had a little quiet time to prepare myself as I best could for to-morrow. But this was not to be. When I got home, the landlord met me in the passage. He was in liquor, and more brutal and pitiless in his way of looking and speaking than ever I saw him before.

"So you're going to be fool enough to pay for her funeral,

are you?" were his first words to me.

I was too weary and heart-sick to answer—I only tried to get by him to my own door.

"If you can pay for burying her," he went on, putting himself in front of me, "you can pay her lawful debts. She owes me three weeks' rent. Suppose you raise the money for that next, and hand it over to me? I am not joking, I can promise you. I mean to have my rent; and if somebody don't pay it, I'll have her body seized and sent to the workhouse!"

Between terror and disgust, I thought I should have dropped to the floor at his feet. But I determined not to let him see how he had horrified me, if I could possibly control myself. So I mastered resolution enough to answer that I did not believe the Law gave him any such wicked power over the dead.

"I'll teach you what the Law is!" he broke in. "You'll raise money to bury her like a born lady when she's died in my debt, will you? And you think I'll let my rights be trampled upon like that, do you? See if I do! I'll give you till to-night to think about it. If I don't have the three weeks she owes, before to-morrow—dead or alive, she shall go to the workhouse!"

This time I managed to push by him and get to my own room, and lock the door in his face. As soon as I was alone, I fell into a breathless, suffocating fit of crying, that seemed to be shaking me to pieces. But there was no good and no help in tears. I did my best to calm myself after a little while, and tried to think whom I should run to for help and protection.

The doctor was the first friend I thought of, but I knew he was always out seeing his patients of an afternoon. The beadle was the next person who came into my head. He had the look of being a very dignified, unapproachable kind of man when he came about the inquest; but he talked to me a little then, and said I was a good girl, and seemed, I really thought, to pity me. So to him I determined to apply in my great danger and distress.

Most fortunately, I found him at home. When I told him of the landlord's infamous threats, and of the misery I was suffering in consequence of them, he rose up with a stamp of his foot, and sent for his gold-laced cocked hat that he wears on Sundays and his long cane with the ivory top to it.

"I'll give it to him," said the beadle. "Come along with me, my dear. I think I told you you were a good girl at the inquest–if I didn't, I tell you so now. I'll give it to him! Come along with me."

And he went out, striding along, with his cocked hat and his great cane, and I followed him.

"Landlord!" he cries, the moment he gets into the passage, with a thump of his cane on the floor. "Landlord!" with a look all round him as if he was king of England calling to a beast. "Come out!"

The moment the landlord came out and saw who it was his eyes fixed on the cocked hat, and he turned as pale as ashes.

"How dare you frighten this poor girl?" says the beadle. "How dare you bully her at this sorrowful time with threatening to do what you know you can't do? How dare you be a cowardly bullying braggadocio of an unmanly landlord? Don't talk to me—I won't hear you! I'll pull you up, sir! If you say another word to the young woman, I'll pull you up before the authorities of this metropolitan parish! I've had my eye on you, and the authorities have had their eye on you, and the rector has had his eye on you. We don't like the look of your small shop round the corner; we don't like the look of some of the customers who deal at it; we don't like disorderly characters; and we don't, by any manner of means, like *you*. Leave the young woman alone, or I'll pull you up! If he says another word, or interferes with you again, my dear, come and tell me; and, as sure as he's a bullying, unmanly braggadocio of a landlord, I'll pull him up!"

With those words, the beadle gave a loud cough to clear his throat and another thump of his cane on the floor, and so went striding out again, before I could open my lips to thank him. The landlord slunk back into his room without a word.

I was left alone and unmolested at last, to strengthen myself for the hard trial of my poor love's funeral to-morrow.

MARCH 13TH.

It is all over. A week ago, her head rested on my bosom. It is laid in the churchyard now–the fresh earth lies heavy over her grave. I, and my dearest friend, the sister of my love, are parted in this world for ever.

I followed her funeral alone through the cruel, bustling streets. Sally, I thought, might have offered to go with me, but she never so much as came into my room. I did not like to think badly of her for this, and I am glad I restrained myself–for, when we got into the churchyard, among the two or three people who were standing by the open grave, I saw Sally, in her ragged grey shawl and her patched black bonnet. She did not seem to notice me till the last words of the service had been read and the clergyman had gone away. Then she came up and spoke to me.

"I couldn't follow along with you," she said, looking at her ragged shawl, "for I haven't a decent suit of clothes to walk in. I wish I could get vent in crying for her like you, but I can't; all the crying's been drudged and starved out of me, long ago. Don't you think about lighting your fire when you get home. I'll do that, and get you a drop of tea to comfort you."

She seemed on the point of saying a kind word or two more; when, seeing the beadle coming towards me, she drew back as if she was afraid of him, and left the churchyard.

"Here's my subscription towards the funeral," said the beadle, giving me back his shilling fee. "Don't say anything about it, for it mightn't be approved of in a business point of view, if it came to some people's ears. Has the landlord said anything more to you? No, I thought not. He's too polite a man to give me the trouble of pulling him up. Don't stop crying here, my dear. Take the advice of a man familiar with funerals, and go home."

I tried to take his advice, but it seemed like deserting Mary to go away when all the rest forsook her.

I waited about till the earth was thrown in and the men had left the place–then I returned to the grave. Oh, how bare and cruel it was, without so much as a bit of green turf to soften it! Oh, how much harder it seemed to live than to die, when I stood alone looking at the heavy piled-up lumps of clay, and thinking of what was hidden beneath them.

I was driven home by my own despairing thoughts. The sight of Sally lighting the fire in my room eased my heart a little. When she was gone, I took up Robert's letter again to keep my mind employed on the only subject in the world that has any interest for me now.

This fresh reading increased the doubts I had already felt relative to his having remained in America after writing to me. My grief and forlornness have made a strange alteration in my former feelings about his coming back. I seem to have lost all my prudence and self-denial, and to care so little about his poverty and so much about himself, that the prospect of his return is really the only comforting thought I have now to support me. I know this is weak in me, and that his coming back poor can lead to no good result for either of us. But he is the only living being left me to love, and—I can't explain it—but I want to put my arms round his neck and tell him about Mary.

MARCH 14TH.

I locked up the end of the cravat in my writing-desk. No change in the dreadful suspicions that the bare sight of it rouses in me. I tremble if I so much as touch it.

MARCH 15TH, 16TH, 17TH.

Work, work, work. If I don't knock up, I shall be able to pay back the advance in another week, and then, with a little more pinching in my daily expenses, I may succeed in saving a shilling or two to get some turf to put over Mary's grave—

and perhaps even a few flowers besides to grow round it.

MARCH 18TH.

Thinking of Robert all day long. Does this mean that he is really coming back? If it does, reckoning the distance he is at from New York, and the time ships take to get to England, I might see him by the end of April or the beginning of May.

MARCH 19TH.

I don't remember my mind running once on the end of the cravat yesterday, and I am certain I never looked at it, yet I had the strangest dream concerning it at night. I thought it was lengthened into a long clue, like the silken thread that led to Rosamond's Bower. I thought I took hold of it, and followed it a little way, and then got frightened and tried to go back but found that I was obliged, in spite of myself, to go on. It led me through a place like the Valley of the Shadow of Death, in an old print I remember in my mother's copy of the *Pilgrim's Progress*. I seemed to be months and months following it without any respite, till at last it brought me, on a sudden, face to face with an angel whose eyes were like Mary's. He said to me:

"Go on, still; the truth is at the end, waiting for you to find it." I burst out crying, for the angel had Mary's voice as well as Mary's eyes, and woke with my heart throbbing, and my cheeks all wet. What is the meaning of this? Is it always superstitious, I wonder, to believe that dreams may come true?

APRIL 30TH.

I have found it! God knows to what results it may lead, but it is as certain as that I am sitting here before my journal, that I have found the cravat from which the end in Mary's hand was torn! I discovered it last night; but the flutter I was in, and the nervousness and uncertainty I felt, prevented me from noting down this most extraordinary and unexpected event at the time when it happened. Let me try if I can preserve the memory of it in writing now.

I was going home rather late from where I work, when I suddenly remembered that I had forgotten to buy myself any candles the evening before and that I should be left in the dark if I did not manage to rectify this mistake in some way. The shop close to me, at which I usually deal, would be shut up, I knew, before I could get to it; so I determined to go into the first place I passed where candles were sold. This turned out to be a small shop with two counters, which did business on one side in the general grocery way, and on the other in the rag and bottle and old iron line.

There were several customers on the grocery side when I went in, so I waited on the empty rag side till I could be served. Glancing about me here at the worthless-looking things by which I was surrounded, my eye was caught by a bundle of rags lying on the counter, as if they had just been brought in and left there. From mere idle curiosity, I looked close at the rags, and saw among them something like an old cravat. I took it up directly and held it under a gas-light. The pattern was blurred lilac lines, running across and across the dingy black ground in a trellis-work form. I looked at the ends; one of them was torn off.

How I managed to hide the breathless surprise into which this discovery threw me, I cannot say, but I certainly contrived to steady my voice somehow and to ask for my candles calmly, when the man and woman serving in the shop, having disposed of their other customers, inquired of me what I wanted.

As the man took down the candles, my brain was all in a whirl with trying to think how I could get possession of the old cravat without exciting any suspicion. Chance, and a little quickness on my part in taking advantage of it, put the object within my reach in a moment. The man, having counted out the candles, asked the woman for some paper to wrap them in. She produced a piece much too small and flimsy for the purpose, and declared, when he called for something better, that the day's supply of stout paper was all exhausted. He flew into a rage with her for managing so badly. Just as they were beginning to quarrel violently, I stepped back to the rag-counter, took the old cravat carelessly out of the bundle, and said, in as light a tone as I could possibly assume:

"Come, come! don't let my candles be the cause of hard words between you. Tie this ragged old thing round them with a bit of string, and I shall carry them home quite comfortably."

The man seemed disposed to insist on the stout paper being produced; but the woman, as if she was glad of an opportunity of spiting him, snatched the candles away and tied them up in a moment in the torn old cravat. I was afraid he would have struck her before my face, he seemed in such a fury, but, fortunately, another customer came in, and obliged him to put his hands to peaceable and proper uses.

"Quite a bundle of all sorts on the opposite counter there," I said to the woman, as I paid her for the candles.

"Yes, and all hoarded up for sale by a poor creature with a lazy brute of a husband, who lets his wife do all the work, while he spends all the money," answered the woman, with a malicious look at the man by her side.

"He can't surely have much money to spend, if his wife has no better work to do than picking up rags," said I.

"It isn't her fault if she hasn't got no better," says the woman, rather angrily. "She's ready to turn her hand to anything. Charring, washing, laying-out, keeping empty houses–nothing comes amiss to her. She's my half-sister, and I think I ought to know."

"Did you say she went out charring?" I asked, making believe as if I knew of somebody who might employ her.

"Yes, of course I did," answered the woman; "and if you can put a job into her hands, you'll be doing a good turn to a poor hard-working creature as wants it. She lives down the mews here to the right–name of Horlick, and as honest a woman as ever stood in shoe-leather. Now then, ma'am, what for you?"

Another customer came in just then and occupied her attention. I left the shop, passed the turning that led down to the Mews, looked up at the name of the street, so as to know how to find it again, and then ran home as fast as I could. Perhaps it was the remembrance of my strange dream striking me on a sudden, or perhaps it was the shock of the discovery I had just made, but I began to feel frightened, without knowing why, and anxious to be under shelter in my own room.

If Robert should come back! Oh, what a relief and help it would be now if Robert should come back!

MAY 1ST.

On getting indoors last night, the first thing I did, after striking a light, was to take the ragged cravat off the candles, and smooth it out on the table. I then took the end that had been in poor Mary's hand out of my writing-desk, and smoothed that out, too. It matched the torn side of the cravat exactly. I put them together, and satisfied myself that there was not a doubt of it.

Not once did I close my eyes that night. A kind of fever got possession of me—a vehement yearning to go on from this first discovery and find out more, no matter what the risk might be. The cravat now really became, to my mind, the clue that I thought I saw in my dream—the clue that I was resolved to follow. I determined to go to Mrs. Horlick this evening, on my return from work.

I found the Mews easily. A crook-backed dwarf of a man was lounging at the corner of it, smoking his pipe. Not liking his looks, I did not inquire of him where Mrs. Horlick lived, but went down the Mews till I met with a woman, and asked her. She directed me to the right number. I knocked at the door, and Mrs. Horlick herself—a lean, ill-tempered, miserable-looking woman—answered it. I told her at once that I had come to ask what her terms were for charring. She stared at me for a moment, then answered my question civilly enough.

"You look surprised at a stranger like me finding you out," I said. "I first came to hear of you last night, from a relation of yours, in rather an odd way."

And I told her all that had happened in the chandler's shop, bringing in the bundle of rags, and the circumstance of my carrying home the candles in the old torn cravat, as often as possible.

"It's the first time I've heard of anything belonging to *him* turning out any use," said Mrs. Horlick, bitterly.

"What, the spoilt old neck-handkerchief belonged to your husband, did it?" said I at a venture.

"Yes; I pitched his rotten rag of a neck-'andkercher into the bundle along with the rest; and I wish I could have pitched him in after it," said Mrs. Horlick. "I'd sell him cheap at any rag-shop. There he stands, smoking his pipe at the end of the Mews, out of work for weeks past, the idlest humpbacked pig in all London!"

She pointed to the man whom I had passed on entering the Mews. My cheeks began to burn and my knees to tremble, for I knew that in tracing the cravat to its owner I was advancing a step towards a fresh discovery. I wished Mrs. Horlick good evening, and said I would write and mention the day on which I wanted her.

"What I had just been told, put a thought into my mind

that I was afraid to follow out. I have heard people talk of being light-headed, and I felt as I have heard them say they felt, when I retraced my steps up the Mews. My head got giddy and my eyes seemed able to see nothing but the figure of the little crook-backed man, still smoking his pipe in his former place, I could see nothing but that; I could think of nothing but the mark of the blow on my poor lost Mary's temple. I know that I must have been light-headed, for as I came close to the crook-backed man, I stopped without meaning it. The minute before, there had been no idea in me of speaking to him. I did not know how to speak, or in what way it would be safest to begin. And yet, the moment I came face to face with him, something out of myself seemed to stop me, and to make me speak without considering beforehand, without thinking of consequences; without knowing, I may almost say, what words I was uttering till the instant when they rose to my lips.

"When your old neck-tie was torn, did you know that one end of it went to the rag-shop, and the other fell into my hands?"

I said these bold words to him suddenly, and, as it seemed, without my own will taking any part in them.

He started, stared, changed colour. He was too much amazed by my sudden speaking to find an answer for me. When he did open his lips, it was to say, rather to himself

41

than me:

"You're not the girl."

"No," I said, with a strange choking at my heart. "I'm her friend."

By this time he had recovered his surprise, and he seemed to be aware that he had let out more than he ought.

"You may be anybody's friend you like," he said brutally, "so long as you don't come jabbering nonsense here. I don't know you, and I don't understand your jokes."

He turned quickly away from me when he had said the last words. He had never once looked fairly at me since I first spoke to him.

Was it his hand that had struck the blow?

I had only sixpence in my pocket, but I took it out and followed him. If it had been a five-pound note, I should have done the same in the state I was in then.

"Would a pot of beer help you to understand me?" I said, and offered him the sixpence.

"A pot ain't no great things," he answered, taking the sixpence doubtfully.

"It may lead to something better," I said.

His eyes began to twinkle, and he came close to me. Oh, how my legs trembled!—How my head swam!

"This is all in a friendly way, is it?" he asked in a whisper.

I nodded my head. At that moment, I could not have

spoken for worlds.

"Friendly, of course," he went on to himself, "or there would have been a policeman in it. She told you, I suppose, that I wasn't the man?"

I nodded my head again. It was all I could do to keep myself standing upright.

"I suppose it's a case of threatening to have him up, and make him settle it quietly for a pound or two? How much for me if you lay hold of him?"

"Half."

I began to be afraid that he would suspect something if I was still silent. The wretch's eyes twinkled again, and he came closer.

"I drove him to the Red Lion, corner of Dodd Street and Rudgely Street. The house was shut up, but he was let in at the jug and bottle-door, like a man who was known to the landlord. That's as much as I can tell you, and I'm certain I'm right. He was the last fare I took up at night. The next morning master give me the sack. Said I cribbed his corn and his fares. I wish I had!"

I gathered from this that the crook-backed man had been a cab-driver.

"Why don't you speak?" he asked suspiciously. "Has she been telling you a pack of lies about me? What did she say when she came home?"

"What ought she to have said?"

"She ought to have said my fare was drunk, and she came in the way as he was going to get into the cab. That's what she ought to have said, to begin with."

"But after."

"Well, after, my fare, by way of larking with her, puts out his leg for to trip her up, and she stumbles and catches at me for to save herself, and tears off one of the limp ends of my rotten old tie. 'What do you mean by that, you brute?' says she, turning round, as soon as she was steady on her legs, to my fare. Says my fare to her: 'I means to teach you to keep a civil tongue in your head.' And he ups with his fist, and–what's come to you, now? What are you looking at me like that for? How do you think a man of my size was to take her part, against a man big enough to have eaten me up? Look as much as you like, in my place you would have done what I done–drove off when he shook his fist at you, and swore he'd be the death of you if you didn't start your horse in no time."

I saw he was working himself up into a rage; but I could not, if my life had depended on it, have stood near him or looked at him any longer. I just managed to stammer out that I had been walking a long way, and that, not being used to much exercise, I felt faint and giddy with fatigue. He only changed from angry to sulky when I made that excuse. I got a little further away from him, and then added that if he would be at the Mews entrance the next evening, I should have something more to say, and something more to give him. He grumbled a few suspicious words in answer, about doubting whether he should trust me to come back. Fortunately, at that moment, a policeman passed on the opposite side of the way. He slunk down the Mews immediately, and I was free to make my escape.

How I got home, I can't say, except that I think I ran the greater part of the way. Sally opened the door, and asked if anything was the matter the moment she saw my face. I answered:

"Nothing! nothing." She stopped me as I was going into my room, and said:

"Smooth your hair a bit, and put your collar straight. There's a gentleman in there waiting for you."

My heart gave one great bound–I knew who it was in an instant, and rushed into the room like a mad woman.

"Oh, Robert! Robert!"

All my heart went out to him in those two little words.

"Good God, Anne! has anything happened? Are you ill?"

"Mary! my poor, lost, murdered, dear, dear Mary!"

That was all I could say before I fell on his breast.

MAY 2ND.

Misfortunes and disappointments have saddened him a little, but towards me he is unaltered. He is as good, as kind, as gently and truly affectionate as ever. I believe no other man in the world could have listened to the story of Mary's death with such tenderness and pity as he. Instead of cutting me short anywhere, he drew me on to tell more than I had intended; and his first generous words, when I had done, were to assure me that he would see himself to the grass being laid and the flowers planted on Mary's grave. I could almost have gone on my knees and worshipped him when he made me that promise.

Surely, this best, and kindest, and noblest of men cannot always be unfortunate. My cheeks burn when I think that he has come back with only a few pounds in his pocket, after all his hard and honest struggles to do well in America. They must be bad people there, when such a man as Robert cannot get on among them. He now talks calmly and resignedly of trying for any one of the lowest employments by which a man can earn his bread honestly in this great city–he who knows French, who can write so beautifully! Oh, if the people who have places to give away only knew Robert as well as I do, what a salary he would have, what a post he would be chosen to occupy!

I am writing these lines alone, while he has gone to the Mews to treat with the dastardly, heartless wretch with whom I spoke yesterday.

Robert says the creature–I won't call him a man–must be humoured and kept deceived about poor Mary's end, in order that we may discover and bring to justice the monster whose drunken blow was the death of her. I shall know no ease of mind till her murderer is secured and till I am certain that he will be made to suffer for his crimes. I wanted to go with Robert to the Mews, but he said it was best that he should carry out the rest of the investigation alone, for my strength and resolution had been too hardly taxed already. He said more words in praise of me for what I have been able to do up to this time, which I am almost ashamed to write down with my own pen. Besides, there is no need–praise from his lips is one of the things that I can trust my memory to preserve to the latest day of my life.

MAY 3RD.

Robert was very long last night before he came back to tell me what he had done. He easily recognized the hunchback at the corner of the Mews by my description of him; but he found it a hard matter, even with the help of money, to overcome the cowardly wretch's distrust of him as a stranger and a man. However, when this had been accomplished, the main difficulty was conquered. The hunchback, excited by the promise of more money, went at once to the Red Lion to inquire about the person whom he had driven there in his cab. Robert followed him and waited at the corner of the street. The tidings brought by the cabman were of the most unexpected kind. The murderer–I can write of him by no other name–had fallen ill on the very night when he was driven to the Red Lion, had taken to his bed there and then, and was still confined to it at that very moment. His disease was of a kind that is brought on by excessive drinking, and that affects the mind as well as the body. The people at the public house called it the Horrors.

Hearing these things, Robert determined to see if he could not find out something more for himself, by going and inquiring at the public house in the character of one of the friends of the sick man in bed upstairs. He made two important discoveries. First, he found out the name and address of the doctor in attendance. Secondly, he entrapped the barman into mentioning the murderous wretch by his name. This last discovery adds an unspeakably fearful interest to the dreadful misfortune of Mary's death. Noah Truscott, as she told me herself in the last conversation I ever had with her, was the name of the man whose drunken example ruined her father; and Noah Truscott is also the name of the man whose drunken fury killed her. There is something that makes one shudder, something supernatural in this awful fact. Robert agrees with me that the hand of Providence must have guided my steps to that shop from which all the discoveries since made took their rise. He says he believes we are the instruments of effecting a righteous retribution; and, if he spends his last farthing, he will have the investigation brought to its full end in a court of justice.

MAY 4TH.

Robert went to-day to consult a lawyer whom he knew in former times. The lawyer was much interested, though not so seriously impressed as he ought to have been by the story of Mary's death and of the events that have followed it. He gave Robert a confidential letter to take to the doctor in attendance on the double-dyed villain at the Red Lion. Robert left the letter, and called again and saw the doctor, who said his patient was getting better and would most likely be up again in ten days or a fortnight. This statement Robert communicated to the lawyer, and the lawyer has undertaken to have the public house properly watched, and the hunchback (who is the most important witness) sharply looked after for the next fortnight, or longer, if necessary.

Here, then, the progress of this dreadful business stops for awhile.

MAY 5TH.

Robert has got a little temporary employment in copying for his friend the lawyer. I am working harder than ever at my needle to make up for the time that has been lost lately.

MAY 6TH.

To-day was Sunday, and Robert proposed that we should go and look at Mary's grave. He, who forgets nothing where a kindness is to be done, has found time to perform the promise he made to me on the night when we first met. The grave is already, by his orders, covered with turf and planted round with shrubs. Some flowers and a low headstone are to be added to make the place look worthier of my poor lost darling who is beneath it. Oh! I hope I shall live long after I am married to Robert! I want so much time to show him all my gratitude!

MAY 20TH.

A hard trial to my courage to-day. I have given evidence at the police office, and have seen the monster who murdered her.

I could only look at him once. I could just see that he was a giant in size, and that he kept his dull, lowering, bestial face turned towards the witness box, and his bloodshot, vacant eyes staring on me. For an instant I tried to confront that look; for an instant I kept my attention fixed on him, on his blotched face, on the short grizzled hair above it–on his knotty, murderous right hand, hanging loose over the bar in front of him, like the paw of a wild beast over the edge of its den. Then the horror of him–the double horror of confronting him in the first place, and afterwards of seeing that he was an old man–overcame me, and I turned away, fain, sick, and shuddering. I never faced him again, and at the end of my evidence Robert considerately took me out.

When we met once more at the end of the examination, Robert told me that the prisoner never spoke and never changed his position. He was either fortified by the cruel composure of a savage or his faculties had not yet thoroughly recovered from the disease that had so lately shaken them. The magistrate seemed to doubt if he was in his right mind; but the evidence of the medical man relieved him from this uncertainty, and the prisoner was committed for trial on a charge of manslaughter.

Why not on a charge of murder? Robert explained the law to me when I asked that question. I accepted the explanation, but it did not satisfy me. Mary Mallinson was killed by a blow from the hand of Noah Truscott. That is murder in the sight of God. Why not murder in the sight of the Law also?

JUNE 18TH.

To-morrow is the day appointed for the trial at the Old Bailey.

Before sunset this evening, I went to look at Mary's grave. The turf has grown so green since I saw it last and the flowers are springing up so prettily. A bird was perched, dressing his feathers, on the low white head-stone that bears the inscription of her name and age. I did not go near enough to disturb the little creature. He looked innocent and pretty on the grave, as Mary herself was in her life-time. When he flew away, I went and sat for a little by the headstone, and read the mournful lines on it. Oh! my love! my love! what harm or wrong had you ever done in this world, that you should die at eighteen by a blow from a drunkard's hand?

JUNE 19TH.

The trial. My experience of what happened at it is limited, like my experience of the examination at the police office, to the time occupied in giving my own evidence. They made me say much more than I said before the magistrate. Between examination and cross-examination, I had to go into almost all the particulars about poor Mary and her funeral that I have written in this journal; the jury listening to every word I spoke with the most anxious attention. At the end, the judge said a few words to me approving of my conduct, and then there was a clapping of hands among the people in court. I was so agitated and excited that I trembled all over when they let me go out into the air again.

I looked at the prisoner both when I entered the witness-box and when I left it. The lowering brutality of his face was unchanged, but his faculties seemed to be more alive and observant than they were at the police office. A frightful blue change passed over his face; and he drew his breath so heavily that the gasps were distinctly audible, while I mentioned Mary by name and described the mark of the blow on her temple. When they asked me if I knew anything of the prisoner, and I answered that I only knew what Mary herself had told me about his having been her father's ruin, he gave a kind of groan and struck both his hands heavily on

53

the dock. And when I passed beneath him on my way out of court, he leaned over suddenly, whether to speak to me or to strike me I can't say, for he was immediately made to stand upright again by the turnkeys on either side of him. While the evidence proceeded (as Robert described it to me), the signs that he was suffering under superstitious terror became more and more apparent, until, at last, just as the lawyer appointed to defend him was rising to speak, he suddenly cried out, in a voice that startled everyone, up to the very judge on the bench:

"Stop!"

There was a pause, and all eyes looked at him. The perspiration was pouring over his face like water, and he made strange, uncouth signs with his hands to the judge opposite. "Stop all this!" he cried out. "I've been the ruin of the father and the death of the child. Hang me before I do more harm! Hang me, for God's sake, out of the way!" As soon as the shock produced by this extraordinary interruption had subsided, he was removed, and there followed a long discussion about whether he was of sound mind, or not. The matter was left to the jury to decide by their verdict. They found him guilty of the charge of manslaughter, without the excuse of insanity. He was brought up again, and condemned to transportation for life. All he did, on hearing the dreadful sentence, was to reiterate his desperate words:

"Hang me before I do more harm! Hang me, for God's sake, out of the way!"

JUNE 20TH.

I made yesterday's entry in sadness of heart, and I have not been better in my spirits to-day. It is something to have brought the murderer to the punishment that he deserves. But the knowledge that this most righteous act of retribution is accomplished brings no consolation with it. The Law does indeed punish Noah Truscott for his crime, but can it raise up Mary Mallinson from her last resting-place in the churchyard?

While writing of the Law, I ought to record that the heartless wretch who allowed Mary to be struck down in his presence without making an attempt to defend her, is not likely to escape with perfect impunity. The policeman who looked after him, to insure his attendance at the trial, discovered that he had committed past offences for which the Law can make him answer. A summons was executed upon him, and he was taken before the magistrate the moment he left the court after giving his evidence.

I had just written these few lines, and was closing my journal, when there came a knock at the door. I answered it, thinking Robert had called on his way home to say good-night, and found myself face to face with a strange gentleman who immediately asked for Anne Rodway. On hearing that I was the person inquired for, he requested five minutes' conversation with me. I showed him into the little empty room at the back of the house and waited, rather surprised and fluttered, to hear what he had to say.

He was a dark man, with a serious manner and a short, stern way of speaking. I was certain that he was a stranger, and yet there seemed something in his face not unfamiliar to me. He began by taking a newspaper from his pocket and asking me if I was the person who had given evidence at the trial of Noah Truscott on a charge of manslaughter? I answered immediately that I was.

"I have been for nearly two years in London, seeking Mary Mallinson, and always seeking her in vain," he said. "The first and only news I have had of her is found in the report of the trial yesterday."

He still spoke calmly, but there was something in the look of his eyes which showed me that he was suffering in spirit. A sudden nervousness overcame me, and I was obliged to sit down.

"You knew Mary Mallinson, sir?" I asked, as quietly as I could.

"I am her brother."

I clasped my hands, and hid my face in despair. Oh, the

bitterness of heart with which I heard him say those simple words.

"You were very kind to her," said the calm, tearless man. "In her name, and for her sake, I thank you."

"Oh, sir," I said, "why did you never write to her when you were in foreign parts?"

"I wrote often," he answered, "but each of my letters contained a remittance of money. Did Mary tell you she had a stepmother? If she did, you may guess why none of my letters were allowed to reach her. I now know that this woman robbed my sister. Has she lied in telling me that she was never informed of Mary's place of abode?"

I remembered that Mary had never communicated with her stepmother after the separation, and could therefore assure him that the woman had spoken the truth.

He paused for a moment after that, and sighed. Then he took out a pocket-book, and said:

"I have already arranged for the payment of any legal expenses that may have been incurred by the trial, but I have still to reimburse you for the funeral charges which you so generously defrayed. Excuse my speaking bluntly on this subject; I am accustomed to look on all matters where money is concerned purely as matters of business."

I saw that he was taking several bank-notes out of the pocket-book, and stopped him.

"I will gratefully receive back the little money I actually paid, sir, because I am not well off, and it would be an ungracious act of pride in me to refuse it from you," I said. "But I see you handling bank-notes, any one of which is far beyond the amount you have to repay me. Pray put them back, sir. What I did for your poor lost sister, I did from my love and fondness for her. You have thanked me for that; and your thanks are all I can receive."

He had hitherto concealed his feelings, but I saw them now begin to get the better of him. His eyes softened, and he took my hand and squeezed it hard.

"I beg your pardon," he said. "I beg your pardon, with all my heart."

There was silence between us, for I was crying; and I believe, at heart, he was crying, too. At last, he dropped my hand, and seemed to change back, by an effort, to his former calmness.

"Is there no one belonging to you to whom I can be of service?" he asked. "I see among the witnesses on the trial the name of a young man who appears to have assisted you in the inquiries which led to the prisoner's conviction. Is he a relation?"

"No, sir; at least, not now—but I hope—"

"What?"

"I hope that he may, one day, be the nearest and dearest

relation to me that a woman can have." I said those words boldly, because I was afraid of his otherwise taking some wrong view of the connection between Robert and me.

"One day?" he repeated. "One day may be a long time hence."

"We are neither of us well off, sir," I said. "One day means the day when we are a little richer than we are now."

"Is the young man educated? Can he produce testimonials to his character? Oblige me by writing his name and address down on the back of that card."

When I had obeyed, in a handwriting which I am afraid did me no credit, he took out another card and gave it to me.

"I shall leave England to-morrow," he said. "There is nothing now to keep me in my own country. If you are ever in any difficulty or distress (which, I pray God, you may never be), apply to my London agent, whose address you have there."

He stopped, and looked at me attentively–then took my hand again.

"Where is she buried?" he said suddenly, in a quick whisper, turning his head away.

I told him, and added that we had made the grave as beautiful as we could with grass and flowers.

I saw his lips whiten and tremble.

"God bless and reward you!" he said, and drew me towards him quickly, and kissed my forehead. I was quite overcome, and sank down and hid my face on the table. When I looked up again, he was gone.

JUNE 25TH,

1841. I write these lines on my wedding morning, when little more than a year has passed since Robert returned to England.

His salary was increased yesterday to one hundred and fifty pounds a year. If I only knew where Mr. Mallinson was, I would write and tell him of our present happiness. But for the situation which his kindness procured for Robert, we might still have been waiting vainly for the day that has now come.

I am to work at home for the future, and Sally is to help us in our new abode. If Mary could have lived to see this day! I am not ungrateful for my blessings; but, oh, how I miss that sweet face, on this morning of all others!

I got up to-day early enough to go alone to the grave, and to gather the nosegay that now lies before me from the flowers that grow round it. I shall put it in my bosom when

Robert comes to fetch me to the church. Mary would have been my bridesmaid if she had lived; and I can't forget Mary, even on my wedding day!

Lightning Source UK Ltd.
Milton Keynes UK
UKHW011321151121
394003UK00002B/493